THOMAS THE TANK ENGINE & FRIENDS
ANNUAL

Based on The Railway Series by The Rev. W. Awdry

Written By Christopher Awdry
© William Heinemann Limited 1990

Cover illustration by Owain Bell
© Britt Allcroft (Thomas) Limited 1986

Endpaper illustration by Owain Bell
© Britt Allcroft (Thomas) Limited 1986

Illustrations for pages 12-13, 16-17, 32-33, 44-45, 48-49, 58-59 by Owain Bell
© Britt Allcroft (Thomas) Limited 1986

Other full colour and line illustrations by David Palmer(Temple Rogers)
© Britt Allcroft (Thomas) Limited 1990

Photographic stills by David Mitton and Terry Permane from Britt Allcroft's production of
"Thomas The Tank Engine and Friends"
© Britt Allcroft (Thomas) Limited 1986

Published by
GRANDREAMS LIMITED
Jadwin House,
205/211 Kentish Town Road,
London NW5 2JU.

Printed in Spain

ISBN 0 86227 784 1

CONTENTS

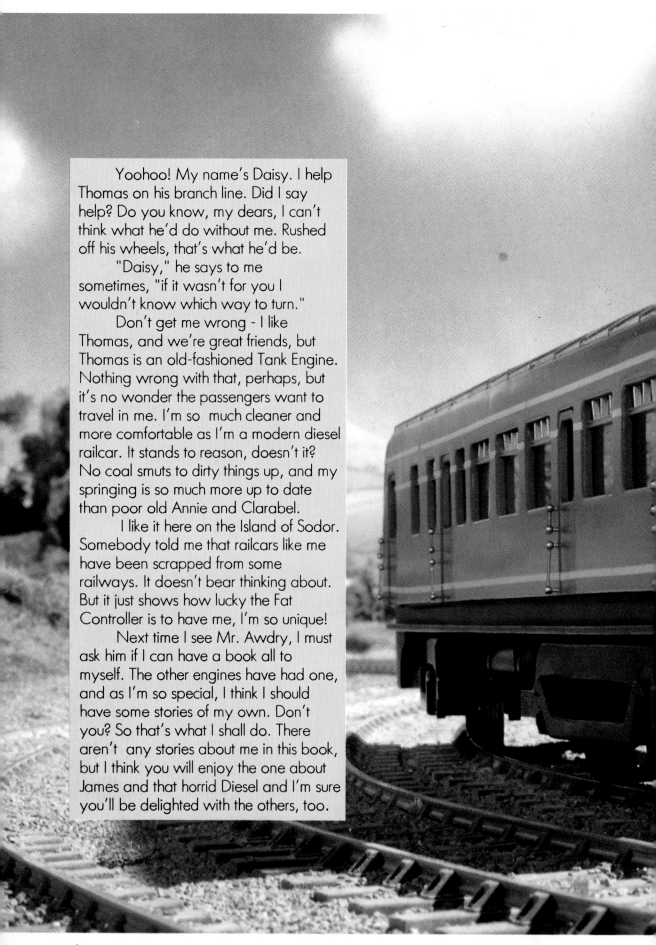

Yoohoo! My name's Daisy. I help Thomas on his branch line. Did I say help? Do you know, my dears, I can't think what he'd do without me. Rushed off his wheels, that's what he'd be.

"Daisy," he says to me sometimes, "if it wasn't for you I wouldn't know which way to turn."

Don't get me wrong - I like Thomas, and we're great friends, but Thomas is an old-fashioned Tank Engine. Nothing wrong with that, perhaps, but it's no wonder the passengers want to travel in me. I'm so much cleaner and more comfortable as I'm a modern diesel railcar. It stands to reason, doesn't it? No coal smuts to dirty things up, and my springing is so much more up to date than poor old Annie and Clarabel.

I like it here on the Island of Sodor. Somebody told me that railcars like me have been scrapped from some railways. It doesn't bear thinking about. But it just shows how lucky the Fat Controller is to have me, I'm so unique!

Next time I see Mr. Awdry, I must ask him if I can have a book all to myself. The other engines have had one, and as I'm so special, I think I should have some stories of my own. Don't you? So that's what I shall do. There aren't any stories about me in this book, but I think you will enjoy the one about James and that horrid Diesel and I'm sure you'll be delighted with the others, too.

NEAR MISS

Near to where the line from the big engine Shed joins the main line there are some special points. They are called trap-points, and the rails don't go anywhere, but are just long enough to derail anything running away and prevent it from colliding with engines on the main line. They are worked by a very powerful spring, but can be controlled from the signalbox when the engines need to join the main line on purpose.

Henry could never understand why they were there.

"Useless things," he grumbled. "They can take them away as soon as they like. Run away indeed! Why should we want to run away from our nice warm shed, tell me that!"

Neither Gordon nor James could, so they didn't bother to try.

One night Henry was alone in the Shed. This was unusual, but Gordon was not due back until early in the morning, and James had been delayed by the Other Railway. Oliver, Donald and Douglas with Duck, were all busy at the other end of Duck and Oliver's branch line.

It was a cold night, and Henry felt lonely. He was glad when the firelighter came earlier

than usual. Gratefully Henry felt warmth spread through his boiler. He was drowsy and comfortable.

"Running away," he thought to himself as he dozed. "Who'd be daft enough to do that on a cold morning like this?"

Suddenly he awoke. Someone was climbing the steps to his cab.

It was the firelighter, who thought it would be fun, while no-one was about, to drive an engine. He unwound the brake and moved the regulator, but nothing happened. Disappointed, the firelighter went away, without closing the regulator.

Henry dozed again. When he next woke he could see that it was just getting light outside. Then he realised what had woken him - steam was trickling into his cylinders.

"It's too early," he thought. "Driver can't be here yet."

Henry felt himself moving. He tried to stop, but he couldn't without his driver and fireman. He tried to whistle - he couldn't do that either. He neared the shed door. It hadn't been built to stop engines. Henry wished it had.

"Ouch!" he exclaimed as he demolished it. It was cold and frosty outside. "Help!" thought Henry as he rumbled along. "I don't like this."

But there was nothing he could do about it. Then he

remembered the main line.

"Horrors!" he thought, "I hope nothing's coming."

A green signal-light, and the sound of an engine approaching, told him that something was coming.

"Help!" thought Henry again. He shut his eyes and waited for the crash.

Just then his front wheels slid to one side. Soon his driving wheels left the rails too, and Henry stopped, leaning a little to one side. He was just a few inches clear of Gordon's coaches, as, with a whistle, a rattle and a roar, the big blue engine thundered by.

"Phew, that was a near miss!" hissed Henry, as men shouted and began to run towards him. "Thank you trap-points - you you can stay there just as long as you like!"

WORD SEARCH 1

Listed below are 18 characters associated with Thomas The Tank Engine. The names are all hidden in the grid. How many can you find? All the words can be found in straight lines - but they can be in any direction. Answers on pages 60-61.

THOMAS   HENRY   EDWARD
DUCK   DONALD   DOUGLAS
ANNIE   TOBY   CLARABEL
BILL   BEN   DIESEL
DAISY   JAMES   GORDON
TREVOR   TERENCE   PERCY

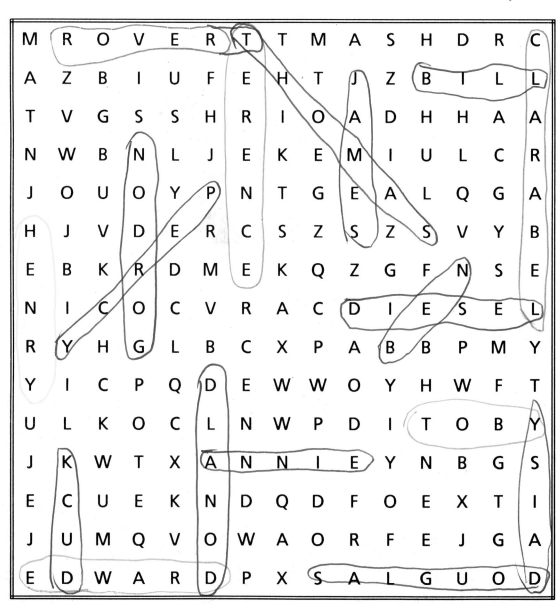

M	R	O	V	E	R	T	T	M	A	S	H	D	R	C
A	Z	B	I	U	F	E	H	T	J	Z	B	I	L	L
T	V	G	S	S	H	R	I	O	A	D	H	H	A	A
N	W	B	N	L	J	E	K	E	M	I	U	L	C	R
J	O	U	O	Y	P	N	T	G	E	A	L	Q	G	A
H	J	V	D	E	R	C	S	Z	S	Z	S	V	Y	B
E	B	K	R	D	M	E	K	Q	Z	G	F	N	S	E
N	I	C	O	C	V	R	A	C	D	I	E	S	E	L
R	Y	H	G	L	B	C	X	P	A	B	B	P	M	Y
Y	I	C	P	Q	D	E	W	W	O	Y	H	W	F	T
U	L	K	O	C	L	N	W	P	D	I	T	O	B	Y
J	K	W	T	X	A	N	N	I	E	Y	N	B	G	S
E	C	U	E	K	N	D	Q	D	F	O	E	X	T	I
J	U	M	Q	V	O	W	A	O	R	F	E	J	G	A
E	D	W	A	R	D	P	X	S	A	L	G	U	O	D

14

A PICTURE TO PAINT

Some of the naughtiest trucks on the whole Railway live at the Works. This is where the engines are mended, so, as you can imagine, there is lots of rubbish to be transported. Every so often, one of the engines has to take the scrap-iron to the yard, where Edward first met Trevor before he moved to the Vicarage orchard. The engines nicknamed the train, 'The Scrap'.

None of the engines liked the job. The trucks were old, rude and noisy - they took absolutely no notice of anything that was said to them (this is not unusual, but these trucks were worse than most), and they made every engine's journey a misery.

One day Boco found that he was to take 'The Scrap'.

"Right," he said to Douglas, who happened to be in the Shed with him. "I'm having no nonsense from those trucks - they'll come quietly or else!"

"Aye," smiled Douglas. "Show 'em who's boss."

The trucks objected to Boco because he was a diesel.

"What's this green thing?" they asked. "A caterpillar?"

Then they accused Boco of bumping them - it was what they deserved, but Boco had been very careful with the trucks. Finally they pretended their brakes were still on, and screamed horribly when

Boco tried to move them.

At last Boco had had enough.

"Right," he said to the trucks. "Any more nonsense, and this trip to the scrapyard will be your last. I'll leave you there to be cut up with the other old iron if you don't start behaving."

The trucks were silent for the first time that morning. But not for long.

One of the oldest trucks began to complain that it felt ill. Boco didn't believe it, but the trucks made such a fuss that he had to do something. Growling fiercely Boco moved around the other trucks and coupled up to the old truck who was grumbling terribly.

"Come on, you," grunted Boco. "Move!"

But before they had moved an inch, there was a splintering noise.

"Ow!" screeched the truck. Suddenly its floor gave way. The scrap iron it was carrying fell through and landed with a loud crash on the rails below.

"Ooooer!" groaned the poor old truck, and collapsed.

So Boco really did have to leave a truck to be broken up for the next scrap-train. The other trucks were very worried as they didn't want to be turned into scrap.

They were quiet and helpful for the rest of the day and it was the easiest run Boco ever had with 'The Scrap'.

21

22

A PICTURE TO PAINT

23

THOMAS'S CROSSWORD

ACROSS

1. These are not popular with some of the engines
4. You find this along the coast
5. This means to cut the grass
6. A goods-carrying motor vehicle
7. Thomas's number
8. This engine is blue

DOWN

1. Annie and Clarabel ride behind him
2. The - - - - - of hearts stole the tarts
3. He is Scottish and has a twin
4. Sometimes used in a duel

Answers on pages 60-61

JOIN THE DOTS

On the day of the Sunday School outing, the stationmaster came to see Thomas.

"Bertie has broken down," he said. "The Fat Controller wants you to run a special train."

"But they're going to the mountains," objected Thomas. "Our line doesn't go there."

"No," agreed the driver, "but the electric one does."

Thomas was excited.

"I've never been along there," he said.

It seemed only a few minutes before the Vicar appeared, followed by a crowd of excited, chattering children. They all got into Annie and Clarabel, the Guard blew his whistle, and

26

Thomas set off.

At the junction Thomas ran round Annie and Clarabel. He whistled cheerfully as he passed Edward's station. Edward was so surprised to see him that he nearly forgot to reply.

They went up Gordon's Hill in great style, and at the next junction, Thomas ran round the coaches again. Poor Annie and Clarabel grew confused.

"Which way are we supposed to be going?" they wondered.

But Thomas was enjoying himself, and they soon reached the station which the Mountain Engines shared with the electric trains. All Thomas's passengers got out, and

27

the Guard made sure they all knew when they had to be back.

"We have to fit in with other trains along here," he warned them. "If we're late goodness knows what time you'll get home!"

Thomas had a splendid day. He enjoyed talking to the other engines, and was sorry when at last it was time to get ready to go home. His driver and fireman refilled his coal-bunker and watertanks, and then they took Annie and Clarabel to the platform.

They waited and they waited. A quarter of an hour later they were still waiting.

"Come on," fretted Thomas.

"We shall miss our path and have to dawdle all the way home if they don't come soon."

They waited again. Still no one came. Then the signalman walked along the platform.

"I can give you five minutes," he told Thomas's Guard. "After that I shall have to put the next electric in front of you."

There was a shout from the road. The Sunday School party, hot and tired, hurried on to the platform.

"So sorry," apologised the Vicar. "A little boy got lost and we had to look for him."

"Never mind," said Thomas, and hurried his load of tired children home as fast as he could.

PICTOGRAMS

Look at the picture clues closely. By adding or subtracting the letters shown you should find 6 engines associated with Thomas The Tank Engine. Answers on pages 60-61.

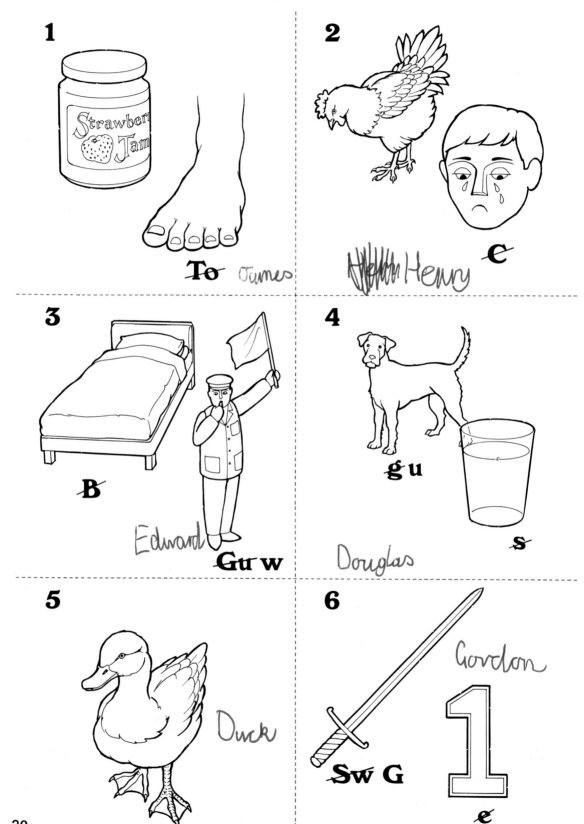

1
To James

2
Henry **c**

3
B Edward **Gu w**

4
gu Douglas **s**

5
Duck

6
Gordon **Sw G** **e**

Can you help DUCK find some water?

A PICTURE TO PAINT

Who can reach the Fat Controller?

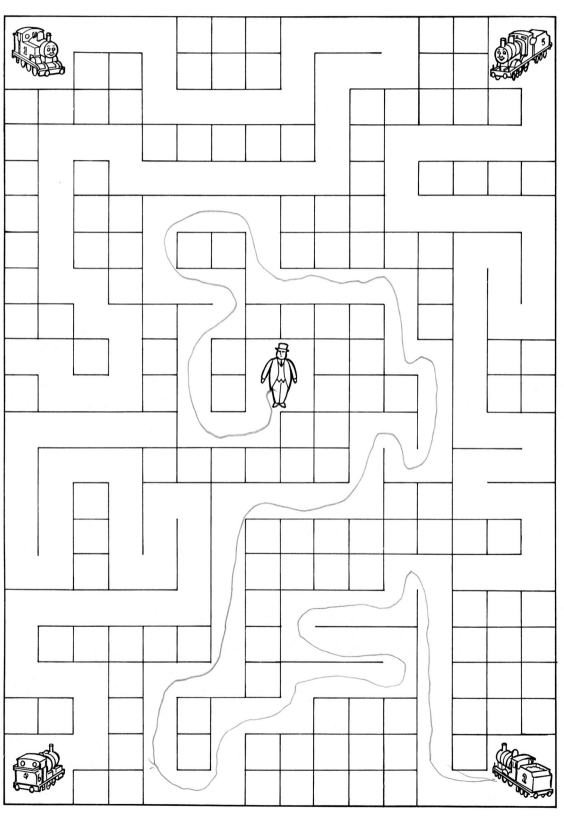

JOIN THE DOTS

IN THE DRINK

Trevor the Traction Engine chuntered happily along the road. He liked unusual jobs, and this one was the sort that he did not often get the chance to do. A farmer had some old cherry trees which didn't give fruit any more, and he had decided to plant new ones in their place. He had telephoned Trevor's owner, the Vicar of Wellsworth, to ask if Trevor could help pull the old trees out of the ground.

"Of course he can," replied the Vicar. "He'll be delighted."

And so, one bright autumn morning, Trevor and his driver, Jem Cole, were making their way to the farm. They had some distance to go, so they had started early,

38

and now, about halfway there, they stopped to refill Trevor's watertank from a roadside stream. It was near the railway, and while Trevor enjoyed his drink, Edward, whistling cheerfully, passed with his first train of the day.

By ten o'clock they reached the farm, and the farmer took them into his orchard. There were three tree stumps to move - the trees, of course, had been felled already.

Trevor's driver used a spade to dig round the first stump, making a hole below the main root. Then he pushed chains through the hole, looped them round and fastened them to the towing bar underneath Trevor's bunker.

"Right," he said to Trevor as he pulled the lever. "Heave!"

Trevor struggled to move forward, pulling hard. There was a creaking noise from the tree stump, but it didn't move.

"Ooof!" panted Trevor. "This is a tough one."

He tried again; this time he felt

39

the stump moving a little. At the third attempt there was a sudden crack. The tree stump came out of the ground in a shower of earth and roots. Trevor jerked forward, the chains clanking and bumping behind him.

"That's one," said his driver. "Well done, Trevor!" Now for number two."

The second stump was no trouble at all, but the third was harder to move than the first had been. By the time it was out of the

ground Trevor felt exhausted.

But the work had taken longer than expected, and there was no time to rest. The autumn evenings were short, and if Trevor and his driver were to get back that day, he had to set off at once, because he had no lights for running on the road.

They stopped when they reached the stream. Trevor's driver placed the hose into the water and opened the valve. Thankfully Trevor sucked the cool water into

his tank.

As the water flowed in, Trevor's tank became heavier. His wheels began to feel unsteady. Suddenly, without warning, the bank on which he was standing slipped sideways towards the stream. Trevor's right-hand wheel sank with it.

"Help!" he gasped. "Look out!"

Jem Cole, who had been watching the hose, jumped clear.

"Ooooer," groaned Trevor, as, slowly, he tilted further and further towards the stream. "I wanted a drink, not a bath!"

But he did not go quite that far. When the ground stopped moving, Trevor's right-hand wheel was about two feet lower than the other one. Quickly Jem put out Trevor's fire, so that his boiler wasn't damaged. Then he let all the water Trevor had just sucked into his tank run away, to make Trevor lighter and less likely to slip again.

"Now what?" asked Trevor anxiously.

"You'll have to be jacked back on to the road," Jem said, "but I need a firm platform to work from."

Edward's branch line lay just ahead. Men were relaying the track, and old sleepers lay on the bank, waiting for Donald to collect them.

"What about those sleepers?" Trevor suggested.

The foreman of the relaying team gave permission, and sent some men to help. First they dug into the bank of the stream, and placed a sleeper below Trevor's wheel, so that he could not slip and, putting the jack on this, slowly raised Trevor, building up both platforms as they did so.

At last Trevor was level again. His driver refilled the boiler and watertank, then relit the fire. It was too late to get home that night, but there was a farm nearby. Jem went to ask if Trevor could spend the night in the farmyard. By the time he came back, Trevor had just enough steam to move safely off the road.

Trevor reached home safely next day. Whenever he goes on a long journey in future, he says, he will be very careful where he stops for a drink.

THE RAILWAY QUIZ

1. Which Twins work at the china clay quarry?

2. What colour is James?

3. Who pulled Thomas out of a snowdrift?

4. Which engine was afraid of a bull?

5. What number is Toby?

6. Do you know Duck's proper name?

7. Who called Henry 'Old Square Wheels'?

8. What is the fish train, sometimes pulled by Henry, called?

9. Which engine is number 9?

10. Who once had a close shave at the barber's?

Answers on pages 60-61.

RUSTY RED SCRAP-IRON

Diesel was very pleased with his nickname for Henry.

"Old Square-Wheels," he chuckled to himself. "Brilliant - suits Henry down to the rails."

The trucks sniggered.

"How clever of Duck to think of it," they said to each other. We know, don't we, that it was really Diesel who had made the name up. But the trucks didn't. Diesel had told them it was Duck, and the trucks believed what they were told.

"Look," they whispered every time Henry went past. "There's Old Square-Wheels."

Henry was furious.

Everyone knew that James disliked diesels, so it was a surprise when Diesel and James got on well together. James showed Diesel where things were in the Yard, and Diesel worked hard once he had settled down. But he was very full of self-importance.

"I'm up-to-date and

revolutionary," he boasted. "I'll soon get this Yard working smoothly."

The trucks hadn't really liked Diesel to start with, and when he began to order them about they liked him even less. But, being trucks, they were sly and didn't show it.

"Keep on the right side of him," they whispered to each other. "We'll get our own back one day."

One morning, James asked Diesel to get some trucks ready for him. "I need the vans on the far side of the Yard," he told Diesel.

But Diesel, full of himself and not listening properly, thought James said: "Leave the vans on the far side of the Yard." So Diesel took no notice of those vans. He collected all the rest and put them ready for James to take away.

When James arrived he found, of course, that he had the wrong train. By this time Diesel was nowhere to be seen.

James hated shunting.

"Where's that Diesel?" he grumbled as he arranged his own train. "Off somewhere being revolutionary, I suppose. Wait till I see him - I'll give him revolution!"

But the delay with the vans made James so late that he could not get back to the Shed that night. This made him even crosser. When he did finally meet Diesel again, Diesel was left in no doubt of what James thought about him.

Diesel slunk away, growling crossly to himself.

"How dare he speak to me like that," he muttered. "Anyone can make a mistake. I'll teach him a lesson, you see if I don't."

Next day Diesel was talking to some trucks in the Yard.

"James has been here a long time," he remarked. "He must be very old."

"Not so old as Edward and

Thomas," replied the trucks. "Thomas was here first, to help build the Railway, but Edward is older. The other engines used to tease him about that, but he proved them wrong."

"How?" asked Diesel.

"It was before I came, even," said one old truck slowly, "but the way I heard it was that one day James ran away - just trundled off down the line without his driver and fireman."

"Good gracious!" exclaimed Diesel. "What happened?"

The truck paused.

"Well," he went on, "Edward was nearby. An Inspector got a cable, and rode on Edward's bufferbeam until Edward caught James up - running on the other line, you see. Then he dropped a loop of cable over James's buffer. They slowed James down with Edward's brakes so that the Inspector could get into James's cab and stop him. They didn't tease Edward after that."

"Quite right," said Diesel. "I bet James felt silly. It's funny, isn't it," he went on. "If James stood out in the rain for a bit, he'd soon be just the colour he is - red with rust."

The trucks sniggered. Suddenly Diesel had an idea. He growled away, looking thoughtful.

"You know that story you told me about James," he said when he saw the trucks again. "I told Duck about it in the Shed, and guess what he said?"

He paused. The trucks waited; they knew Diesel was going to tell them anyway.

"Duck said," Diesel went on impressively, "it was no wonder that Edward caught up with him, because James is only rusty red scrap-iron. Wasn't that rude? But that's what Duck said."

The silly trucks believed every word.

"Tee hee," they tittered. "Wait till we tell the others."

The story went round quickly, and when James next came to the

Yard the trucks laughed rudely at him.
    "Here's Old Scrap-Iron,"
they chortled. "Look at him - just a
heap of rusty red scrap-iron."
    James soon found out why.
His feelings can be imagined.
    "That Duck!" he hissed
furiously. "Let him just wait - I'll
make him duck!"
    Diesel, lurking in the
background, smirked triumphantly.

WORD SEARCH 2

Listed below are 12 things associated with Thomas The Tank Engine. All the words are hidden in the grid. How many can you find? All the words are in a straight line - but can be found in any direction. Answers on pages 60-61.

PLATFORM ✓   STATION ✓   GUARD ✓
SIGNAL ✓   TRUCKS ✓   DRIVER ✓
WHISTLE ✓   FLAG ✓   TICKET ✓
ENGINE ✓   PASSENGERS ✓ STEAM ✓

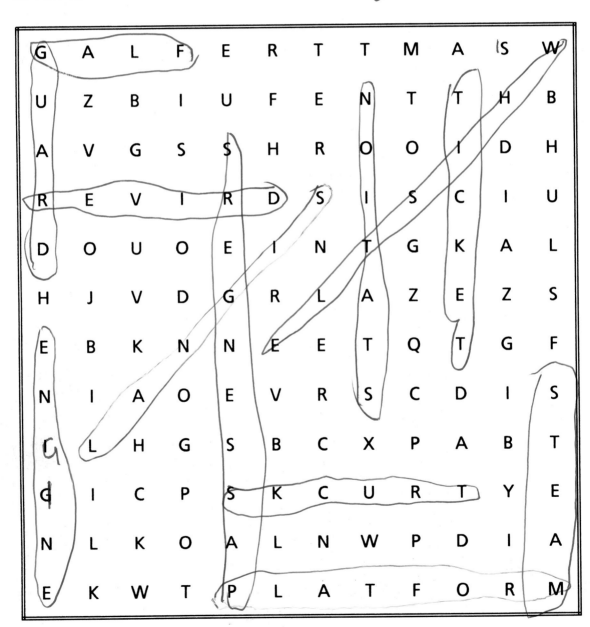

G A L F E R T T M A S W
U Z B I U F E N T T H B
A V G S S H R O O I D H
R E V I R D S I S C I U
D O U O E I N T G K A L
H J V D G R L A Z E Z S
E B K N N E E T Q T G F
N I A O E V R S C D I S
G L H G S B C X P A B T
G I C P S K C U R T Y E
N L K O A L N W P D I A
E K W T P L A T F O R M

ANSWERS

P.14 WORD SEARCH 1

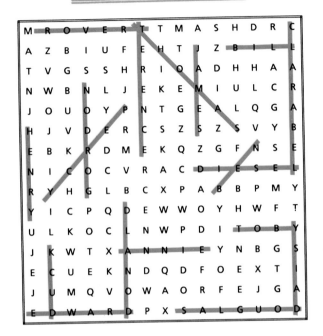

```
M R O V E R T T M A S H D R C
A Z B I U F E H T J Z B I L L
T V G S S H R I O A D H H A I
N W B N L J E K E M I U L C R
J O U O Y P N T G E A L Q G A
H J V D E R C S Z S Z S V Y B
E B K R D M E K Q Z G F N S E
N I C O C V R A C D I E S E L
R Y H G L B C X P A B B P M Y
Y I C P Q D E W W O Y H W F T
U L K O C L N W P D I T O B Y
J K W T X A N N I E Y N B G S
E C U E K N D Q D F O E X T I
J U M Q V O W A O R F E J G A
E D W A R D P X S A L G U O D
```

P.24 THOMAS'S CROSSWORD

```
¹T R U C K ²S
H        N    ³D
O    ⁴S E A    O
⁵M O W    ⁶V A N
A    ⁷O N E    A
A    R        L
  ⁸E D W A R D
```

P.30 PICTOGRAMS

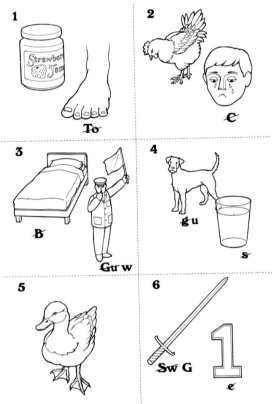

1. JAM (TO)ES = JAMES
2. HEN (C)RY = HENRY
3. (B)ED (GU)WARD = EDWARD
4. DO(G) U GLAS(S) = DOUGLAS
5. DUCK
6. (SW)GORD ON(E) = GORDON

P.31 MAZE

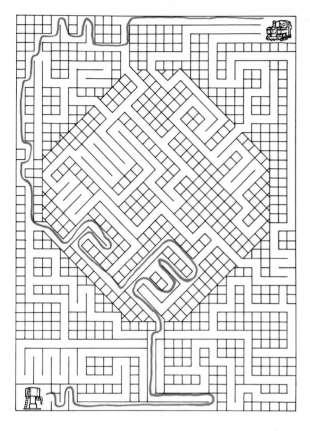

P.46 THE RAILWAY QUIZ

1. BILL AND BEN.
2. RED.
3. TERENCE.
4. DAISY.
5. 7.
6. MONTAGUE.
7. DIESEL.
8. THE FLYING KIPPER.
9. DONALD.
10. DUCK.

P.36 MAZE

P.56 WORD SEARCH 2

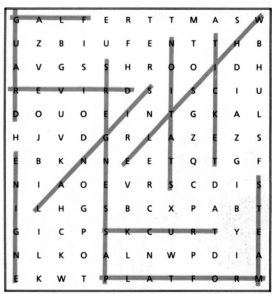